Tons of Trucks!

CAR CARRIERS

By Luke Harasymiw

Gareth Stevens
PUBLISHING

Please visit our website, www.garethstevens.com. For a free color catalog of all our high-quality books, call toll free 1-800-542-2595 or fax 1-877-542-2596.

Cataloging-in-Publication Data

Names: Harasymiw, Luke.
Title: Car carriers / Luke Harasymiw.
Description: New York : Gareth Stevens Publishing, 2020. | Series: Tons of trucks! | Includes index.
Identifiers: ISBN 9781538245019 (pbk.) | ISBN 9781538245033 (library bound) | ISBN 9781538245026 (6 pack)
Subjects: LCSH: Trucks–Juvenile literature. | Trucking–Juvenile literature.
Classification: LCC TL230.15 H297 2020 | DDC 629.224–dc23

First Edition

Published in 2020 by
Gareth Stevens Publishing
111 East 14th Street, Suite 349
New York, NY 10003

Editor: Therese Shea
Designer: Katelyn E. Reynolds

Photo credits: Cover, p. 1 Art Konovalov/Shutterstock.com; p. 5 Imagepocket/Shutterstock.com; p. 7 Mikbiz/Shutterstock.com; p. 9 Vibrant Image Studio/Shutterstock.com; p. 11 onyV3112/Shutterstock.com; pp. 13, 24 (ramp) CC7/Shutterstock.com; pp. 15, 17, 24 (strap) Roman Babakin/Shutterstock.com; p. 19 Mike Kuhlman/Shutterstock.com; p. 21 betto rodrigues/Shutterstock.com; p. 23 klarka0608/Shutterstock.com.

Printed in the United States of America

Contents

This is my toy truck.
It's a car carrier!

Car carriers
carry cars.

Some carry a few cars.
Some carry 12 cars!

Some carry even more!

Cars drive up a ramp. The ramp can move up and down.

The cars won't fall. Chains or straps hold them.

Some car carriers
carry new cars.
Some carry
broken cars.

Some car carriers
are open.
You can see the cars.

Some car carriers
have walls.
They keep the cars safe.

Some tow trucks
are car carriers!
I love trucks!

Words to Know

ramp

strap

Index